This book belongs to

_____

_____

The
Clever Little Rabbit

AND OTHER ANIMAL STORIES

The
Clever Little
Rabbit

AND OTHER ANIMAL STORIES

P
• PARRAGON •

First published in Great Britain in 1998 by
Parragon
13 Whiteladies Road
Clifton
Bristol BS8 1PB

ISBN 0 75252-529-8

Printed in Great Britain

Reprinted in 1999

Produced by Nicola Baxter
PO Box 71
Diss Norfolk IP22 2DT

Stories by Nicola Baxter
Designed by Amanda Hawkes
Text illustrations by Duncan Gutteridge
Cover illustration by Alisa Tingley

Contents

The Clever
Little
Rabbit

Nobody knew how the clever little rabbit came to be quite so clever. His parents were friendly, hardworking rabbits, but no one would have said they were particularly clever. In fact, the clever little rabbit's father got rather muddled if he had to count more than twenty-two cabbages at one time.

The clever little rabbit's brothers and sisters were quite ordinary little rabbits too. Tippytoes was well above average at hopping, but she could never remember if a hundred carrots was more than eight dozen. (It is.)

Twizzler had bigger ears than almost any rabbit you have ever seen, but he got stuck in the alphabet when he reached "f is for fox" (which is, after all, enough to frighten any young rabbit away from his letters.)

So the clever little rabbit's cleverness was a mystery. His name was Albert, but most rabbits called him Cleverclogs.

Before he had left the first class at school, Albert had read all the books in the junior library. Before he had left the second class, he had read all the teachers' books too.

"I'm afraid there is nothing more I can teach your son, Mr Nibbles," the headteacher told Albert's father. "He already knows more about maths and geography and carrot-crunching than I do."

Mr Nibbles was filled with pride, but he did rather wonder what to do with his extra-clever boy. After all, there is only so much maths and geography and carrot-crunching you can use in everyday life.

"Don't worry, Dad," said the clever little rabbit. "I'm setting up an Educational Emporium."

"A what?" asked his father. That sentence had contained at least two words that he didn't understand at all.

"An Educational Emporium," said Albert. "It's like a shop where you can find out all about everything."

"Shop" was a word that Mr Nibbles did understand. "You mean people give you money?" he asked.

"Yes," said Albert. "I hope so."

Mr Nibbles looked puzzled. "But what about stock, Albert?"

he asked. "You know, the stuff you're going to sell. How are you going to be able to buy that?"

"I know what stock is, Dad," laughed Albert. "And I don't have to buy it. It's all right up here." And he tapped his forehead in a mysterious manner.

Mr Nibbles still felt that he did not quite understand what Albert was proposing to do, but he soon found out the next day. In an empty tree-trunk house, Albert opened up his famous Educational Emporium.

His very first customer was his brother Twizzler. "Albert, I can't understand my maths homework

at all," he said. "Can your Ed … Eju … can you help me?"

"Let me have a look," said the clever little rabbit. "Yes, I see. That will be two carrots, please, Twizzler."

The price seemed cheap to Twizzler, who had spent four hours the night before puzzling over his fractions. He willingly handed over the carrots. In two minutes flat, the clever little rabbit had finished the problems and even written them down in something that looked very like Twizzler's paw-writing.

Very soon, most of the children at the school were

coming along to Albert to have their homework checked, finished, or just done from start to finish. Albert enjoyed the work and soon had more carrots, wizzo-balls and sweets than he really knew what to do with.

News of Albert's cleverness spread far and wide. Soon grown-up rabbits began to come to him as well. Old Farmer Fogarty brought over his accounts, which had caused him so much trouble that his whiskers were fraying. Albert took a day or two to sort them out, but Farmer Fogarty was really delighted with the result.

Aunt Jemima asked Albert to adjust her jam recipe, so that it made seventeen jars instead of eleven. The Bunny sisters regularly asked for help with the crossword in their newspaper. Miss Bunnyhop asked Albert to write all her letters to her boyfriend overseas, with the result that she became engaged within two weeks.

As the months and years passed, Albert became an essential part of life in the rabbit realm. There was even talk of calling the town Albertville. Albert was a very rich young rabbit, although to be fair, he hardly noticed how wealthy he had become. He was much more interested in solving problems and using his clever little brain.

One day, something happened to show that Albert's Educational Emporium was perhaps not quite such a good thing as everyone had thought. It was the middle of winter. Snow lay thick on the ground, and most sensible rabbits were snuggled deep in their burrows.

The wind blew and blew, whistling round the fields with an icy chill, blowing whirling snowflakes before it. When the storm finally stopped, the rabbits peeped out of their burrows to look at the strange, white world. It was then that they found that wind had pushed over a tree at the corner of a meadow, blocking the entrance to one large rabbit family's underground home.

Normally, the rabbits inside would have been able to dig themselves out, or the rabbits outside would have been able to dig themselves in, but the ground was so hard, it was quite impossible for any kind of digging to happen.

"We could write a note and push it down between the

branches, so that the rabbits inside know help is on its way," suggested Twizzler, as more and more rabbits gathered by the fallen tree.

"That's a good idea," said Mr Nibbles. "You write it, Twizzler."

But Twizzler looked rather embarrassed. The truth was that since Albert had set up his Educational Emporium, Twizzler hadn't written anything for himself at all. Now he had forgotten how! It soon became clear that none of the other rabbits could remember how to write proper letters either.

"I'll do it," said Albert quietly.

"Now," said Farmer Fogarty, taking charge of the practical side of things, "we're going to need some rope. Let's see. We'll need five metres here, and seven metres here, and fourteen metres for pulling. That makes ... er ... that's ... I never was much good at doing sums in my head."

The truth was that no one did sums at all any more, of course. Albert did them instead.

"We need twenty-six metres of rope," said Albert, thoughtfully.

It wasn't very long before the fallen tree had been pulled away and the trapped rabbits were rescued. The grateful family from the burrow below thanked all the rabbits for their help.

"We couldn't have done it without Albert," said Farmer Fogarty, and all the other rabbits agreed. But Albert seemed to have disappeared.

Next morning, Farmer Fogarty went along to the Educational Emporium to have his seed order written out as usual.

"I've brought a large bag of cabbages," he said. "I take it your charges haven't gone up recently, Albert?"

"No," said Albert, "but they have changed. Instead of a bag of cabbages, Farmer Fogarty, I will need you to do something for me in return for my help."

"What's that?" asked the old farmer in surprise.

"I will need you to help me with your seed order," said Albert. "I shall do some, and you will do some. We can finish it very quickly together."

Farmer Fogarty was doubtful, but by the time they had finished, he had remembered how to spell "seed" and "best" and "barley", so he felt pretty pleased with himself.

Over the weeks and months that followed, Albert helped his neighbours as usual, but he spent as much time showing them how to work out their own problems as he did solving them by himself.

Gradually, fewer and fewer rabbits made their way to Albert's door. The Educational Emporium was empty most of the day, but the rabbits who lived nearby were some of the cleverest rabbits you have ever met. Albert had less and less to do, although he still kept busy reading his books. Sometimes a whole week went by without a single rabbit knocking on the door. You might have thought that Albert would be worried, but he looked as cheerful as ever.

Finally, the day came when Albert put a big sign on the door of the Educational Emporium.

CLOSED

Word flew round the town that Albert had gone out of business. Before the ink was dry on the notice, everyone had gathered outside the door of the famous Emporium to see what could be done to save it.

"We need you, Albert," said Twizzler.

"Why?" asked Albert.

"Well, to … and … or… well, I don't know."

It was true. The rabbits themselves could now do all the sums and letters and problems that Albert had helped with before. They really were very clever little rabbits.

"My job is over," said Albert. "The important thing about being clever is to pass on your cleverness to everyone else. It took me a long time to realise that, but I've been working hard, and I think I've done it now."

"But have you taught us everything you know?" asked Mr Nibbles, remembering an important conversation long ago with Albert's headteacher.

"Well, no," said Albert. "But what else is there that you would *like* to know?"

"I was thinking of Evening Classes," said Mr Nibbles firmly. "I've always had a great wish to learn Chinese. There are a lot of rabbits in China, you know."

"I was thinking of Advanced Carrot Arranging," said Miss Honeybun.

"I would be interested in a course on meaty … meaty-o …

meaty-o-algy," said young Twizzler, hesitantly.

"Meaty-o-algy?"

"You know, about the weather," explained Twizzler.

Albert smiled. "Courses in Chinese, Carrot Arranging and Meteorology will begin next week," he said. "Now, if you will excuse me, I have some studying to do."

You will be glad to know that the Educational Emporium is flourishing, and Albert has never been happier. It takes a very clever little rabbit to solve everyone else's problems, but it takes an even cleverer rabbit to show others how to solve their own problems. And Albert, as you know, was a very clever little rabbit indeed.

The
Unhappy
Elephant

Once upon a time, there was an unhappy elephant. He was so unhappy that all the other animals in the jungle were miserable too.

Early in the morning, the monkeys would be disturbed in their treetops by a big, sad, booming sound.

"Boo hoo! Boo hoo!"

The noise shook the leaves and the mangoes from the trees.

"There goes our breakfast again!" sighed one monkey. "Something has got to be done about that elephant."

In another part of the jungle, high in the branches of a

glubglub tree, the parrots were squawking together.

"What are we going to do about that elephant?" they asked each other. "He's got to cheer up. We can't go on like this."

"Very true, very true," whistled the little singing birds in the branches above.

"Ssssoooo," hissed the tree snake, slithering around a nearby trunk. "What's the trouble with the sssssobbing one?"

For a whole minute, the chattering birds were silent. They were never quite sure if they could trust the slithering snake, who moved so silently.

At last an older parrot shuffled his feet on his perch.

"Well, we don't really know," he said. "It all started a few weeks ago. He was a perfectly happy elephant before that."

"Then I ssssuggest that ssssomeone finds out," said the snake, sliding silently away to find his breakfast.

The birds looked at each other. Then they all spoke at once.

"This is a job for a monkey," they said.

When the wisest monkey of all was told what they wanted, he agreed at once with their unanimous decision.

"You're quite right," he said. "Someone must talk to the poor animal and find out what is wrong. Then, perhaps, we can do something to put it right. But let me have my breakfast first. For this kind of job, I will need to be on top form."

So the monkey munched some mangoes. Then he didn't feel quite ready to face the elephant, so he snacked on a couple of bananas. Still, the idea of talking to a sad elephant wasn't very appealing, so he swung over to another part of the jungle and found some of his favourite green leaves. By the time he had finished those, he was almost too full to do anything.

"I think I'll just have a little sleep," he said, "so that I'll be fresh and my wits will be sharp for talking to that elephant."

The other monkeys sat in their treetops and listened. The sounds of the sad elephant still echoed through the jungle.

"Boo hoo! Boo hoo!"

"It doesn't sound as if anyone is talking to him," said the youngest monkey in a puzzled little voice.

"Excuse me," said the wisest monkey's wife. "I think I know what may have happened." She hurried off across the jungle and found her husband sleeping peacefully in the branches of a glubglub tree. He was not sleeping peacefully for long...

So it was that the wisest monkey had a rather pink face as he swung down into the clearing where the elephant was still sadly sniffling.

"Boo hoo! Boo hoo!" said, the elephant, more quietly now.

The wisest monkey cleared his throat and tried to look kindly and, if not wise, at least reasonably clever. He was very aware that the elephant was several hundred times larger than he was. There were stories in the past of elephants carelessly plonking one of their great feet on a monkey's tail, with tragic results. With this in mind, the wisest monkey stayed well out of the way on a branch level with the elephant's eyes.

"Ahem! I couldn't help noticing, old chap…" began the monkey, scratching himself in a way that was meant to look as if he was relaxed and confident. In fact, to an elephant, it made him look particularly nervous and shifty. The elephant moved his great weight from foot to foot and waited for the monkey to continue. He did not think it was likely that the monkey could have anything interesting to say.

"Well, it isn't just me," said the monkey. "Several of your jungle friends have noticed that you're not … well, that is, you're very … I mean to say, you're a bit…"

"You mean I'm miserable," said the elephant, in a low, rumbling voice that quivered in a rather desperate kind of way.

"Miserable? Yes. Good word. Miserable. That's a fine way of putting it," said the monkey, encouragingly.

"It's not a very fine way of feeling," said the elephant.

"No, no, of course not. Not a fine way of feeling at all. But might I ask … that is, if I could be so bold as to enquire … in fact, I wonder if you would be good enough to tell me…"

"Why I'm so miserable?" asked the large grey animal.

"Yes, yes. That's it exactly." The monkey tried to take a grip and put on his most professional tones. "Now what exactly seems to be the trouble?" he asked.

"I'm too fat," said the elephant.

"What?" The monkey couldn't believe his ears. "Feeling flat, did you say?" he queried. "Everyone does at some time, you know."

"No. I'm too *fat*. Too round. Too heavy. Too solid. Too much of me. Too fat."

"Oh," said the monkey, "that kind of too fat. I see."

But in truth he did not see. Too fat? An elephant? It wasn't possible. Whoever heard of a thin elephant?

"What makes you think so?" he asked at last, a hundred questions still buzzing in his brain.

"It's obvious," replied the elephant. "Name me one animal in the whole wide world who's bigger than me! Have you ever seen one? No, I thought not. How would you like to be the fattest animal on earth? Would that make you happy?"

The wisest monkey really could not think of anything to say to that. The idea of being the fattest monkey on earth was not very appealing. The idea of being an elephant was not appealing either (for they are notoriously bad at climbing trees). On the other hand, the idea of being a fat elephant did not sound so very awful. If you had to be an elephant, surely it was better to be a fat elephant?

As he could think of no reassuring words, the monkey risked a quick pat on the huge elephant's trunk and swung off through the branches to report back to the other animals.

"Well?" asked the parrot. "What's the matter with the old fellow?"

The wisest monkey explained. Then he explained again.

Then, as no one seemed able to believe what he said, he led the parrot and the other monkeys and the little singing birds and the tree snake to the elephant's clearing and let them hear for themselves.

What a twittering and a chattering and a hissing there was! Everyone tried to talk at once, but no one could think of a single sensible thing to say to the elephant.

Except one. The old parrot fluttered on his jewelled wings to a nearby branch and spoke with authority.

"My dear friend," he said, "where would we all be without your majestic size? Who was it who pushed over that tree last year when our smallest monkey got trapped inside the trunk? Who gave a mighty shake to the nuggle-nut tree, so that its nuts came tumbling down from the highest branches? Who frightened away that lean, low leopard when he came visiting only a month ago, looking at little birds and monkeys with his glittering eyes? Who stamped out the first sparks of a dreadful forest fire with his beautiful big feet? It was you, my friend. None of the rest of us could have done any of those things."

"So you think it's all right to be the largest animal on earth?" quavered the elephant, shuffling.

"I'm sorry to tell you," replied the parrot, nodding his rainbow head wisely, "that you are not the largest animal on earth by any means. That great honour – and it is an honour indeed – goes to the blue whale, an animal so huge that it cannot live on land at all. It does not have legs, for no legs could support its mighty size. It swims in the oceans."

"Then how does anyone know it is there?" asked the elephant, curious in spite of himself.

"From time to time," replied the parrot, "the whale rises to the surface of the sea to breathe, for it is not a fish but an animal like ourselves. When it breathes out, a great spurt of water flies up from the top of its head, higher in the air than our highest jungle trees. It comes out with a kind of a woosh!"

"Like the spurting I can do from my trunk?" asked the elephant with interest.

"Very like," said the parrot.

"Then I have a big cousin in the sea," smiled the elephant. "I don't know why you call him a whale, for he is clearly an ocean elephant, the greatest of us all."

"Ha, ha!" agreed the parrot. "You see, my friend, that bigness is nothing to be afraid of at all."

"I see that clearly now," agreed the elephant. "I see, indeed, that I am not too big but too small. If you will excuse me, I must have my breakfast at once. There is some serious eating to be done."

And he wandered happily off in search of fruit and leaves.

"There'll be nothing left for the rest of us," groaned the other animals as soon as he was gone.

"He may even find my secret mango store," agreed the wisest monkey. "Why did you have to open your big beak, parrot? This was quite obviously a job for monkeys!"

"He will be sssstamping his great feet everywhere," hissed the tree snake.

If there is a moral to this story, it is that you can't keep everybody happy all the time. That a monkey is still a monkey, however wise he is. And that we should all feel very happy indeed that blue whales do not have legs. Or there would be no mangoes left for the rest of us – none at all!

The
Sheep
Shambles

You probably know the nursery rhyme about Little Bo Peep. That silly girl lost all her sheep and didn't know where to find them. In the end, they came home again, but not before she had had some very worrying moments and one or two sleepless nights.

Once there was a shepherd who was very, very anxious about losing his sheep. Of course, every shepherd is concerned about this, but young Douglas McDougal had rather a reputation for losing parts of his flock. It wasn't really his fault. Some sheep are just plain contrary, and if they could fall into gullies or get stuck behind boulders, you can be sure that Douglas McDougal's sheep would. He was supposed to have a hundred sheep, but very often one or two of them wandered off for a while.

Luckily, because he was a hardworking shepherd, he usually found them again, but that didn't stop his friends from laughing at him. They called him "Little Bo Peep" and chuckled whenever they saw him. Douglas McDougal was determined he would never have another mishap in all his days on the hillside.

In the summertime, it was not so very difficult. Douglas McDougal and his dog, called Jem, could look out across the green hillside and know that every white dot was a sheep or a lamb. It was quite easy to count them and make sure that there were none missing, especially in the middle of the day, when it was hot. Many sheep are not very energetic animals at the best of times, and in hot weather they are not so keen to run races or jump over streams.

"Ninety-seven, ninety-eight ... don't interrupt me, Jem ... ninety-nine, one hundred! They're all there!" Douglas McDougal would say with a smile, as he sat with his sandwiches under the only tree on the hill.

Then Jem would allow himself ten minutes' snooze in the sunshine, before he ran off to check that none of the stragglers had strayed.

In this way, Douglas McDougal and Jem managed not to lose a

single sheep all summer. In fact, they actually found one that had strayed from another flock, although they returned it at once.

Still Douglas McDougal's friends made fun of him.

"How many sheep have you lost today, Bo Peep?" they would call. "Where's your bonnet?"

Douglas McDougal began to dread the winter, for then the whole hillside was covered with snow. It can be very hard to see a white sheep among the white snow. What was he going to do?

Douglas McDougal thought long and hard. He considered radio transmitters around the sheep's necks. He thought about painting numbers on their backs and hiring a helicopter. He wondered if he could train them to make a specially loud bleating sound so that he could track them down. He considered putting them in fluorescent cycling jackets. He even thought about tying leads to their legs, so that he could pull the bleating strays through the snow towards him.

None of these ideas was really possible. Most of them, to be sure, were rather silly. In the end, Douglas McDougal decided to ask his friend Hamish Hamish for advice.

Now Hamish Hamish was an inventor who lived in Douglas McDougal's village. He had a reputation for being a very clever man. Like many inventors, Hamish Hamish was brimming with ideas. Half of them were brilliant. Half of them were crazy. The really difficult thing was telling which were which. His porridge-pourer, for example, had worked really well, and was used by several of the hotels round about. His haggis-heater, on the other hand, had caused several serious explosions and considerable damage to the roof of the village store.

Still, Douglas McDougal was desperate, so he explained his problem to Hamish Hamish. It didn't take the inventor long to come up with an idea.

"The problem is," he said, "that sheep are white and snow is white."

"I know that," said Douglas McDougal.

"One of them," cried Hamish Hamish, "will have to change."

"You think I should spray the snow a different colour?" asked Douglas McDougal.

"No," replied the inventor. "I think you should change the colour of your sheep."

"Now look," said Douglas McDougal rather heatedly. "One of the reasons I am anxious not to lose any sheep is so that my friends don't laugh at me. What do you think they will say if I suddenly turn up with pink or green sheep? I'd never hear the end of it."

"I was thinking of a lovely shade of turquoise," said Hamish Hamish coldly. "And you wouldn't need to worry about your friends. During the coldest weather, they will be more than busy looking after their own sheep on their own hillsides. No one but you will see your sheep until spring, and by then the colour will have faded away completely."

This sounded quite sensible. "You're quite sure that the colour will disappear?" asked Douglas McDougal.

"It is not affected by wet," said Hamish Hamish, "but it fades to white in warm sunshine. In spring you will have the whitest, brightest sheep anyone in the hills has ever seen."

So Douglas McDougal went home with a packet of powder, which he put in the sheep's water as Hamish Hamish had instructed.

"It won't work at once," said the inventor. "But as soon as the weather becomes really cold, you will see the difference."

Douglas McDougal watched his sheep carefully. They looked just the same as ever. Then, one night, there was a sharp frost. In the morning, when the shepherd went to look at his flock, he saw a hillside covered with little blancmanges. There was no doubt about it. The sheep were pink!

Douglas McDougal left Jem in charge and stormed off to Hamish Hamish's house at once.

"The sheep are not," he said, "a lovely shade of turquoise.

They are pink, and it is not a subtle shade."

"Salmon?" asked Hamish Hamish. "Rose-petal? Blush? Peach?"

"The term I would use," said the shepherd, "is puce."

"Hmmm," said Hamish Hamish, "not quite turquoise then, but still very visible against the snow, and that, after all, is the point of the exercise. Let's not get carried away with irrelevancies, young Douglas."

Young Douglas went back to his sheep, and even he had to admit that he had no trouble keeping track of them that winter. He was interested to see that the new lambs that were born were just as bright a colour as their mothers, so he had no trouble looking after them either.

As winter passed, and the first sunshine of spring began to filter palely through the clouds, Douglas McDougal waited with some anxiety to see what would happen to the colour of his well-tended sheep.

"The change will come any day now," Hamish Hamish assured him. "Have patience, my boy."

One morning, the inventor found Douglas McDougal waiting for him when he drew back his bedroom curtains.

"The change has come," said the shepherd grimly. "I'd like you to come and see."

Without giving the inventor time to change out of his dressing gown, Douglas dragged Hamish Hamish down the road and up into the hills. There,

spread across the hillside, were
Douglas McDougal's sheep. A
finer flock you never did see, and
they were not pink. No, they
were blue and purple and red
and orange and yellow and
green. In fact, they were every
single colour of the rainbow.

"Ah," said the inventor. "Ah,
now, yes, I see."

"What exactly do you see?"
asked the shepherd, icily.

"I see two that are absolutely
the lovely shade of turquoise I
was thinking of," said Hamish
Hamish in a squeaky voice.

"What exactly," asked Douglas
McDougal, in a voice that was, if

anything, even colder, "do you suggest that I do?"

"A hot wash and an extra-long rinse cycle?" queried Hamish Hamish. "Bleach? Little white jackets to cover them from foot to tail? A big shock to turn their hair white? Emigration?"

He was already halfway down the road, as Douglas McDougal raised his shepherd's crook in what can only be described as a threatening manner.

Douglas McDougal knew that it was only a matter of time before his friends climbed up to his hillside and discovered the awful truth about his flock.

But next day, as the young shepherd climbed wearily up to his flock, he was astonished to see that his secret had already been discovered. There seemed to be more people on the hillside than sheep! Several television cameras and a whole crowd of news photographers were crowding round an orange lamb, while men with clipboards tried unsuccessfully to herd sheep of different attractive colours to stand next to each other.

"I need another yellow one!" a man in a tweed jacket was calling. "No, no, the magenta will clash. Oh, all right, blue will do."

As Douglas McDougal approached, a woman in a long scarf ran up to him with a microphone.

"Mr McDougal," she cried, "how does it feel to be named the Young Entrepreneur of the Year for your Ready-Dyed Wool Production?"

"My what?" asked Douglas.

"Your coloured sheep," explained the woman in the scarf. "Have you not heard about your prize?"

It soon became clear that, far from laughing at Douglas McDougal, everyone wanted sheep just like his. Overnight, he was famous, and his sheep were in great demand.

"How did you do it, Douglas?" the news reporters asked him.

"I don't know…" began the shepherd, but Hamish Hamish could be heard behind him.

"It was the result of years of work," he said. "I'm Hamish Hamish, Mr McDougal's Research and Development Officer. How big did you say the prize was?"

Well, Douglas McDougal is a rich man now and is quite happy to be called Little Bo Peep if that is what people want to do, but he still gets a little nervous when the sun shines.

The
Bothering
Buzz

There was once an old man who lived by himself in the country. He had no neighbours for miles around.

"Don't you feel lonely?" asked his sister, when she visited from the town at the end of the valley.

"Not at all," replied Mr Billings. "What I need more than anything else is peace and quiet to do my work. I couldn't have that with neighbours popping in and out all the time, could I?"

"But what if you get ill," his sister went on. "We might not know for weeks and weeks. You could be lying on the floor, moaning and groaning."

"You know perfectly well," her brother replied, "that I'm as strong as an ox. Nothing is going to happen to me, but to put your mind at rest, why don't we have a signal?"

"A signal?" said his sister. "What kind of signal?"

"Your little boy has a brand new telescope, doesn't he?"

"Yes, but what…?"

"Look through the telescope at ten o'clock every morning, and, if I'm not well, I'll light a fire and make a smoke signal. If you see smoke rising from the cottage, you'll know I'm not well – or the cottage is on fire, of course. In

either case, your assistance will
be very gratefully received."

Mr Billings' sister had to be
satisfied with that, but she still
went home shaking her head
over her brother's stubbornness.

Mr Billings went happily back
into his cottage and sat down
with his books. He was writing
an encyclopedia of natural
history, which he knew would
take him years to complete. That
didn't worry Mr Billings. He
enjoyed his work so much that
he looked forward to sitting
down with his books each
morning. Not many people are
lucky enough to be so happy in

their work as Mr Billings, even if he *was* still on "a" for "ant".

Mr Billings' days passed peacefully in his country cottage. He would get up at dawn, when the sun was just peeping over the horizon, and make himself some tea. Then he would go straight to his desk and delve once more into the fascinating world of plants, animals and insects. In fact, he very often forgot to eat his lunch *or* his supper, but he munched happily at the apples that grew on the tree outside his window, and his sister would send him a large fruit cake at least once a week.

Meanwhile, Mr Billings sister was following the plan that he had outlined. Every morning at ten o'clock, she borrowed her son's telescope and peered out of the window with it. She became so skilled that she could pick her brother's cottage out from among the trees in five seconds flat. There never was any smoke curling from the chimney, so she felt happy that Mr Billings was safe and well.

For six months, Mr Billings worked quietly away. He had reached "b" for "barnacles" and was particularly fascinated by the way that barnacles cling on to the bottoms of ships, hitching rides around the world.

One morning, Mr Billings was drawing a map to show the journey of one particularly adventurous barnacle, when his concentration was disturbed by a buzzing sound.

"Buzz! Buzz!" it went, right next to his ear. Mr Billings flapped his hands wildly around his head. It sounded as though there was an insect hovering just behind him.

The buzzing stopped, and Mr Billings continued with his work. But just as he was turning the page of one of his books, he heard the annoying sound again.

"Buzz! Buzz!"

Mr Billings stood up. If there was one thing he needed, it was peace and quiet, and this buzzing was driving him mad. He looked around very, very carefully, using his magnifying glass to search in the corners, and at last he found the cause of the bothering buzz.

A little brown bee was sitting on the edge of his desk.

"Buzz!" it said, in a friendly way. "Buzz!"

"This won't do, you know," said Mr Billings. "This won't do at all. I cannot have my work interrupted by this buzz, buzz, buzzing. Can't you be quieter, little bee?"

The bee did its very, very best. "Buzz!" it said. "Buzz! Buzz!"

But Mr Billings had very sensitive ears. Even when the bee was buzzing as quietly as it knew how, he could still hear it.

"I'm afraid you're going to have to go outside, my friend," said

Mr Billings. "And please try not to come inside my cottage again, because I really don't want to hurt you. You are such a little bee, and I am such a big Billings that it might be a disaster if I sat on you by mistake."

The little bee privately thought that the disaster might not be all on one side. After all, Mr Billings might not feel so cheerful with a sting on his big bottom!

Mr Billings opened the window, and out flew the bee. The kindly old gentleman went back to his work and was soon lost in his undersea world again, where there are no bees at all.

Half an hour later, Mr Billings' work was rudely interrupted.

"Buzz! BUZZ!" came a noise in his ear, much, much louder than last time.

"It's that blessed bee again!" cried Mr Billings, picking up his magnifying glass. This time he found the little creature much more quickly. It was perched right on the end of his pencil!

"Now, you know," said Mr Billings rather angrily, "that you and I discussed this matter only a few minutes ago. And I thought that we had an understanding. Bees outside. Billings inside. That was how it went."

But as Mr Billings looked closely at the bee, he began to feel sure that this was not the same bee that he had talked with before. This bee was a little darker in colour and rather smaller than the first one.

"I'm sorry," said Mr Billings, who did like to be fair when he could, "perhaps we haven't met. But I'm afraid I shall have to tell you what I told your friend. I really cannot have buzzing in my ears when I am working. It is most distressing. Now buzz off like a good little bee and let me get on. And you might like to tell your friends what I have told you."

I'm sure you don't need me to tell you what happened for the rest of the afternoon. Over and over again, Mr Billings was disturbed by a buzz, buzz, buzzing. When he looked at his visitor with his magnifying glass, he was almost sure each time that it was a different bee from the time before.

Of course, it is not easy to recognise different bees, unless you are a bee yourself, so Mr Billings became rather confused before the end of the afternoon. Finally, at his wits' end, he decided to look up the subject of bees in one of his books.

What he read there was not very encouraging. He discovered something that he would have known already if he had paused to think for two minutes earlier that day. Bees do not live alone, as Mr Billings did. They live in swarms of hundreds or maybe thousands of bees, all of them busily bustling and buzzing about all day long.

Mr Billings put down his book. So there was a swarm of bees somewhere very near his cottage. So the bee visitors were very likely to continue. So the buzzing was very *un*likely to stop. Whatever could he do? Mr

Billings went to bed that night with a heavy heart.

"I've been very happy in this little cottage," he said to himself. "I really don't want to have to move away, but what is the alternative? I can't possibly work here with all this buzzing. Wait a minute, perhaps that's the answer! If I am not to move, then the bees must move instead!"

Mr Billings was so excited about his idea that he could not stay in bed. He bounced up and sat late into the night, reading his books about insects.

In the morning, he didn't even wait for his breakfast tea, but set out straight away for the town, to make some special purchases.

Mr Billings returned home that afternoon with a large cardboard box and a small pumping machine. It was too late to begin work that day, but he went to bed confident that his troubles would soon be at an end.

Next morning, Mr Billings searched in his old chests and found his ancient insect-hunting outfit from his days on the Amazon. He put on some gloves, a long-sleeved shirt, long trousers and some boots. Then he put a large hat on his head. It had a net hanging all the way round it, so that insects couldn't creep under it and sting him on the nose!

Ready at last, Mr Billings picked up his cardboard box and his pumping machine and went outside. It did not take very long to find the swarm of bees. Mr Billings simply followed the sound of buzzing until he came to one of his old apple trees. There, high in the branches, Mr Billings could see a huge mass of bees clinging together.

Mr Billings made his last-minute preparations. With the box under one arm and the pumping machine held firmly in

his hand, he began slowly to
climb the ladder leaning against
the tree. Inch by inch, he
climbed, as quietly as a cat.

One or two bees buzzed around to look at this strange creature who was approaching their home, but he looked harmless enough.

As soon as he was near enough to the mass of bees, Mr Billings opened his cardboard box and lodged it safely on a broad branch. Then he pointed his pumping machine at the bees and pumped for all he was worth.

It was a smoke machine. Mr Billings' books had told him that the smoke would make the bees drowsy, so that he could catch them in the box and take them to someone who could look after them in a proper hive. It worked like a charm. The sleepy bees dropped into the box, and even the stray ones followed them, so they were not left behind.

As quickly as he could with his gloved hands, Mr Billings fastened the cardboard box and carried it carefully down the tree. He put it on the back seat of his car while he went inside to change out of his insect-catching clothes and hat.

As he changed, Mr Billings took a deep breath and listened hard. Nothing! Not a buzz could be heard anywhere in the still and silent cottage.

"Peace at last!" said Mr Billings. *Drrrriiiiiiinnnng! Drrrriiiiiiinnnng! Beeeeeebaaaa! Beeeeeebaaaa!"*

An atrocious nose assaulted Mr Billings' ears. It was hundreds of times worse than any buzzing he had ever heard.

Mr Billings was so confused for a moment, he almost didn't notice the hammering on his front door.

When he opened it, he was amazed to see two burly firemen, a policeman and two ambulance drivers standing outside.

"Step aside, Sir," said one of the firemen. "We'll soon have this under control. Which way?"

"Which way to what?" asked Mr Billings.

"To the fire!" said the fireman. "Don't waste our time, please."

"What fire?" cried Mr Billings. "There isn't any fire."

"That's not what this lady says," said the fireman sternly. He moved back to reveal … Mr Billings' sister!

"Oh George," she sobbed. "I thought something dreadful had happened to you."

Yes, that morning, Mr Billings' sister had picked up her son's telescope as usual and looked out towards her brother's cottage. You can imagine her concern when she saw lots and lots of white smoke billowing from the cottage. At least, it looked as if it were coming from the cottage, for, of course, it never entered her head that so much smoke could be coming from an apple tree!

Mr Billings' sister lost no time. She rang up all the emergency services and set off herself at once. She was determined to save her brother at all costs. As she drove along, she couldn't help remembering her brother's little joke. "If you see smoke rising from the cottage, you'll know I'm not well – or the

cottage is on fire, of course."
How little she had dreamed that
his laughing words would come
true! Thank goodness she had
agreed to that silly signal!

Now Mr Billings' quiet cottage
was surrounded by vehicles and
people. *Woooooosh!* a stream of
water flooded through his open
bedroom window (and straight
on to his bed below), as one of
the younger firemen got rather
enthusiastic with the hose.

It took some time for all the
explanations to be made, but
everything worked out quite well
in the end. One of the ambulance
drivers turned out to be an

expert on bees and happily took them away to put in his own hive.

Even the firemen and the policeman were not too cross.

"It's good to do an exercise like this from time to time," said the policeman. "But don't make a habit of it."

When everyone had gone, Mr Billings' sister turned to her brother and apologised.

"It's not your fault, my dear," he said. "I'll go and make us both a nice cup of tea. You'll feel better after that."

Later, as they sat under the apple tree and Mr Billings' sister's knees had almost stopped shaking, he begged her again not to worry.

"You were only trying to look after me," he said. "I'm a very lucky man to have someone like you. But we are going to need a much better signalling system in the future, aren't we?"

"What did you have in mind?" asked his sister anxiously. "It will take me a little while to learn semaphore or morse code. Or were you thinking of something more complicated?"

"Not at all, my dear," laughed Mr Billings. "I was thinking of doing something I should have done months ago. I was thinking of buying a telephone!"

The
Inquisitive
Parrot

Once upon a time, there was a parrot who simply could not mind his own business. If he heard two monkeys discussing their sister's cousin's new baby, he would have to poke his rather large beak right into the private conversation.

"What did they call the baby?" he would squawk. "Evangeline is a nice name, especially for a monkey. Or what about Annabel or Gwendoline?"

The monkeys would shuffle along their branch a little to try to escape from the annoying eavesdropper, but the parrot never noticed hints of that kind.

"Christabel is also a lovely name. My aunt's brother-in-law called his second daughter that. I thought it was terribly pretty. What do you think?"

The monkeys would look at each other in despair. The only way to get rid of the parrot was to be downright rude to him, but no one wants to do that if it can be helped.

"I'm also very fond of Carmelita. So charming. And Madeleine has a very sweet sound, too."

Finally, of course, one of the monkeys would simply have to look the inquisitive parrot in the eye and tell him to mind his own business. "We were having a private conversation," she would say, "and now you have spoilt it, so we are leaving. And just in *case* you're interested, and I'm sure you *will* be, the baby was a boy, and they're calling him Karl."

Do you think the parrot was upset at being spoken to in this way? Did he ruffle his feathers and sidle away, hanging his brilliant green head? Not a bit of it. The whole thing was like water off a … well, off a *parrot's* back. As the monkeys moved off, you might hear him muttering to himself. "Hmmm, Karl. That's not a bad name at all. In fact, I'm sure I remember my mother telling me, oh, it must be years ago now, that her cousin…"

That was how it went on, day after day, deep in the jungle. Now the jungle, as you probably know, is usually a very sociable place. Everyone knows everyone else, and there is more gossip and chattering to be heard among the huge green leaves than almost anywhere else on earth. Of course, some of the larger animals are not such great chatterers – you won't often find a leopard discussing the weather with an elephant, for example –

but most of the time, the animals all get along together pretty well.

Perhaps that is why the other animals put up with the parrot as well as they did. He was an incredibly nosey bird, but he didn't really mean any harm by it. It was simply that if there was something going on, then he had to know about it. And he wouldn't rest until he had found out, even if everyone was quite determined to keep the secret.

The trouble with secrets, as I'm sure you know, is that they are really no good at all unless you can *tell* someone about them. I mean, what is the use of knowing a particularly good secret if you can't let someone else know that you know it? And then, of course, once they know that you know something, they will not rest until you have told *them* too.

"Well, I will tell *you*," we say, "but you must promise me not to tell anyone else at all."

It never quite works, does it? That someone has to tell just one other someone, and so on, and so on.

That was why the parrot really didn't have too much trouble finding out about everything that was going on, whether the others wanted him to know or not.

One day, one of the little singing birds who lived at the top of the nuggle-nut tree discovered a very important secret indeed. The elephant whose big grey shape could often be seen wandering across the jungle clearings was about to have a birthday, and it was rather an important birthday, too. He was going to be seventy years old, which is a very great age for an elephant, and certainly something that should be celebrated.

"We should have a party," said the little singing birds. "And all the animals will be invited. We'll

pick some beautiful flowers to make into a garland for the elephant. He will look so very handsome with it round his neck."

"We can collect lots of lovely green leaves for everyone to eat," said the monkeys, "and some nuts and fruit as well, of course."

"What about a birthday song?" asked the singing birds, who, as you can see, were really entering into the spirit of the occasion. "We could sing a special Happy Birthday song for him."

"We're not very good at singing," said the monkeys, "but we could put on an acrobatic display, swooping through the branches while you sang your song, perhaps. What do you think? Would he like that?"

It was generally agreed that the elephant would like that very much indeed.

Then one of the monkeys said what several of the animals had been thinking.

"Er … it *is* supposed to be a surprise, isn't it?" she asked.

"Yes," agreed the singing birds, all twittering together. "The elephant mustn't know anything about it until the great day."

"So that means," said the monkey, "that we must be very, very careful not to let him know, even by the slightest little hint. We will need to very careful."

Everyone could see where the conversation was leading. One little monkey was brave enough to say it.

"So we are agreed, then, that the parrot must not be told about this. Am I right?"

There was no shortage of voices to agree with *that*. Of course, agreeing *not* to do something is much, much easier than putting the agreement into practice. Over and over again, during the weeks that followed, the parrot would just happen to be around when something

important was being discussed.
It was quite obvious to him that
a Really Big Secret was lurking
somewhere in the jungle, and he
felt quite sure it was his duty to
find it.

The parrot found his first clue
late one night, when the stars
were twinkling in the dark sky
above the trees. At night the
jungle is full of sounds.

As the parrot looked up at the night sky, he heard a little chirping sound far above him. As quietly as he could, he hopped up through the branches until he was nearer to the sound. It was very, very soft, but he thought he heard, floating through the dark leaves, just a few words.

"Happy Birthday, dear hmmm hmm hmm, Happy Birthday to youuuoooo!"

The parrot shook his head. It wasn't anybody's birthday today, surely? And anyway, why would those little singing birds be celebrating a birthday in the middle of the night? They were usually fast asleep by this time.

Unless … unless they were practising! That must be it. They were practising a birthday song for someone very special.

The parrot pecked thoughtfully at his feathers. He couldn't think of anyone who had a birthday about now. In fact, like most animals, he couldn't even remember when his own birthday was. It is usually only animals who are very good at remembering things – such as elephants – who celebrate their birthdays at all.

The parrot wished he could creep closer to the little singing birds, but he was afraid of being heard. He was a rather large parrot and not very good at creeping silently through the leaves. Besides, the branches at the top of the trees were very, very, thin. He thought they might well not bear the weight of a rather plump parrot.

Next morning, as he was going about his business as usual (which really means, as he was going about putting his beak into everyone else's business), the parrot was nearly knocked off his perch by a monkey swinging by.

Woooosh! Just as he regained his balance, another one hurtled past, and *Woooooosh! Wooooosh!*

Woooooosh! another and another and another.

The parrot scuttled down to a fallen log near the ground, where he felt safer. What on earth was going on? Those monkeys were well known to be rather lazy in the mornings. Here they were swooping and wooping through thebranches as though they were showing off to someone very important.

Just then, the parrot heard one of the monkeys call to another, high up above his head.

"If you start your swing a little earlier, I can catch you just as you pass over you-know-who's head. It will look much more impressive. Trust me!"

"All right," called another monkey. "But if you drop me, you can peel your own bananas from now on!"

The parrot hopped up and down with excitement. Those monkeys were putting on a show! They were going to do a special performance for someone very important. Whoever could it be?

The parrot thought and thought. Perhaps a famous animal of some kind was going to visit the jungle. But in that case, why didn't he know about it? The more the parrot thought, the more he felt sure that the other animals were deliberately keeping secrets not just from anyone, but from *him*! It seemed very strange.

That night, the parrot could not sleep. In his mind, he kept going over and over the clues he had picked up. From something a baby monkey had let slip, he felt sure that the great event was to happen the following afternoon. What could it be?

It was then that the parrot suddenly hit upon a solution that would explain why he was the last to know about the surprise birthday treat. It must be his *own* birthday! That was the only possible reason for all this secrecy. The animals were going to surprise him!

Now, if he had stopped to think about it a little more, the parrot might have realised that if he didn't know himself when his birthday was, the chances were that the other animals wouldn't know either. But he didn't stop to think. He was so filled up with pride and excitement that not another sensible thought went through his feathery head the whole night.

Next morning, the parrot was beside himself with excitement.

There was hustling and bustling everywhere, as all the animals prepared their various suprises. The parrot peered round leaves and peeped under branches, but he only saw the most tantalising glimpses of what was being done. He wondered where he should spend the rest of the morning. He didn't, after all, want to make it difficult for the other animals to *find* him when the time came. With that in mind, the parrot went to sit right in the middle of the biggest clearing in the jungle, which was, in fact, the very one that the animals had chosen for the elephant's party.

"What's he doing sssssitting *there*?" hissed the tree snake. "He's in the way as usssssual. What are we going to do?"

"Someone will have to have a word with him," said one of the monkeys. "It's probably time he was told, anyway. He can't really do anything to spoil it all now. My cousin is making sure the elephant has a long, muddy bath this morning, so that he doesn't come back and find out what's going on."

The monkey swung down into the clearing and ambled over to the parrot, who was trying to look casual, as though he sat around in the middle of an open space every day of the week.

"Hello, there," said the monkey. "A word in your ear, old friend. There's something we think you should know."

"No, no," said the parrot, blushing and holding up a wing. "You don't have to say anything. I've guessed your secret already, and I must say, I think it's a wonderful idea. I'm very touched. Very touched, indeed."

"Are you?" asked the monkey, surprised. He hadn't realised that the parrot was quite so fond of the elephant. After all, there had been that time when he got squirted by mistake and had to spend a whole week drying out his feathers.

"So ... er ... were you thinking of waiting here until..." began the monkey. "Because there are one or two things we need to get ready, you know."

"Oh," squawked the parrot. "Yes, of course. I'm sorry. I'm in the way. I'll come back, shall I, this afternoon?"

"That would be perfect," said the monkey. "Don't be late!"

"Oh, I wouldn't dream of it," chuckled the parrot. Late for his own party? Of course not! What a day this was going to be!

True to his word, the parrot stayed away until the afternoon. He gave his feathers a special preening and polished his beak on the bark of a tree. Then he strutted back to the clearing.

It looked beautiful. There were garlands of colourful flowers stretched between the trees, and all the animals of the jungle were gathered around. In the centre, there was a big space for the guest of honour. In fact, a very big space indeed for a parrot.

As the parrot entered, a great cheer went up. The parrot tried to look modest, as all the animals broke into song together.

"Happy Birthday to you,
Happy Birthday to you,
Happy Birthday, dear ELEPHANT!
Happy Birthday to you!"

WHAT? The parrot fell off his perch as the elephant came into the clearing. It wasn't his own birthday at all!

After the elephant's party, the parrot was a changed bird. No longer did he listen to gossip or try to find out other animals' secrets. In fact, he's the kind of parrot you might not mind telling a secret to yourself nowadays – well, *almost*.

The
Reserve
Reindeer

Have you ever wondered what would happen if one of Santa Claus' reindeer couldn't pull the sleigh one Christmas? What if one of them had a pulled muscle or a bad cold? There are a lot of nasty germs about at that time of year. The answer is that there is always a reserve reindeer – a reindeer who waits patiently in his stable over Christmas in case one of the other reindeer is a little off colour.

Now being a reserve reindeer is a little like being the understudy for a leading role in a play. Although it is very good to be a part of everything, and they wouldn't want anything bad to happen to *anyone*, most under-studies can't help hoping at one time or another that something will happen to the leading actor or actress. Not anything really serious, of course. Just a little bit of a sore throat, or the tiniest sprained ankle. After all, every understudy needs a chance to show the rest of the world just what he or she is made of.

Reindeer are no different. There was once a reserve reindeer who longed for the chance to fly with the other reindeer, pulling Santa's sleigh across the sky and delivering parcels to children all over the world who have been good.

"It must be wonderful," the reserve reindeer would sigh, "to give pleasure to so many little ones every year."

"It's hard work," said one reindeer, who had been in the first team for several years.

"It's dreadfully cold," said another, munching some hay.

"You've no idea how heavy that sleigh is when we set off," said a third. "And as you know, we have to return several times to fill it up again during the night."

"It's not a job for youngsters," said the fourth reindeer. "You need to be big, fit and strong for this job."

The reserve reindeer listened in silence. He was sure that everything they were saying was true, but even so, he wanted more than anything to help Santa.

But on Christmas Eve, when Santa went out to make the final check of the reindeer, every one of them seemed to be in top condition. The old man in red ran his hands along their backs and down their legs. He made sure that their antlers weren't wobbly and their noses were as cold as they should be. Then he pronounced them all fit and ready for work. There was no place for the reserve reindeer.

The reserve reindeer watched as the first team were buckled into their harnesses. Santa's elves had nimble little fingers, used to doing up each one of the complicated straps and buckles.

The sleigh was already loaded for the first time, piled high with presents for children in every city and each little country cottage.

Finally, Santa went round and had a quiet word with each of the reindeer in turn, giving them each a special piece of apple or a favourite sweet to encourage them in the difficult task ahead.

As the old man climbed into the sleigh and picked up the reins, the reserve reindeer felt the same excitement he experienced every year. Even if he was not part of the team, it was a wonderful sight to see the huge sleigh and the powerful reindeer go hurtling over the snow. Faster and faster they went until, with a *woosh!* they left the ground and flew up into the cold, starlit sky.

The reserve reindeer watched until the sleigh could no longer be seen, then he went back into his warm stable and settled down for a few hours.

Three times during the night, the sleigh returned to be filled again. Each time, the reserve reindeer went out and watched as the reindeer were given water and food to prepare them for the next stage of their great journey.

At last the final presents were loaded into the sleigh.

"Here we go on our last trip for this year!" called Santa. "Up, up

and away, my brave reindeer.
Just one more journey to make!"

Once again, the sleigh
wooshed away over the snow,
before lifting into the night sky.
The little reindeer felt a little sad
as he turned back towards his
stable. It was almost over for
another year.

But as he crossed the snowy
yard to his stable, the reserve
reindeer noticed something that
Santa, busy as he was, had not.
A small pile of presents had
fallen off the sleigh and into a
little pile of snow, where they
had been hidden from Santa and
his elves.

The reserve reindeer wandered over to the presents and looked at them. They were beautifully wrapped in gold, red and green paper. Santa had certainly meant to take them with him.

The little reindeer wondered what to do. When Santa and the reindeer returned from their last trip, it would be almost morning and far too late to make another delivery. But Santa wouldn't want even one child to be disappointed this Christmas.

"There's only one thing to do," said the little reindeer to himself. "I'll have to deliver these presents myself. Now where are those elves hiding?"

The reserve reindeer knew that he could not carry out his plan without the help of the elves. Quickly, he knocked on the window of Santa's home with his nose, so that the elves opened the window and asked him what he wanted. It took the reserve reindeer no time at all to explain.

When they understood the problem, some of the elves

looked rather guilty. It was their job, after all, to make sure that no presents were left behind. They were only too eager to help the reserve reindeer to put the mistake right. But how was he going to carry those presents? There were not very many of them, but reindeer do not have hands to carry things, and they need all four of their feet for walking or flying.

At last, one of the older elves thought of a little elf-sleigh at the back of the sleigh shed. It was quickly brought out and dusted down – just big enough for a pile of presents and one little elf.

In no time at all, the reserve reindeer found himself strapped into the sleigh. The presents were loaded, and the oldest elf stepped forward to take his seat.

"No," said the reserve reindeer. "If you don't mind, Sir, I would rather take a young elf, who is not so heavy. This is my first flight, you know."

The elves understood at once and choose a young but very sensible elf called Jingle.

"Are you ready?" called the reserve reindeer, feeling a kind of wobbly feeling in his tummy. "It's time to go. Climb on board now. It will soon be morning!"

Now the reserve reindeer had never flown even a few feet before. He knew that the magic of Christmas night would make it possible for him to fly, but even so, his heart was in his mouth as he set off across the snow at a brisk trot. Faster and faster he went, on and on. Just when he thought that he could not go any faster, he felt a strange sensation under his hooves and saw that he was several metres above the earth. He was flying!

The reserve reindeer looked back over his shoulder. "All right back there?" he called to the little elf who was clinging on behind.

"Fine!" called the excited young elf. "I think we need to swing to the left here!"

The reindeer really had no idea how to make turns in mid-air, but as soon as he *thought* about turning, he found he was doing it!

It was all going much better than the reserve reindeer had hoped, but he could feel the cold air whistling through his coat, and already his hooves were feeling tired and heavy.

"That house down there!" called the elf from the back, pointing out a small cottage with a tall chimney. To his surprise, the reindeer saw that he had flown over several towns and villages without noticing.

Carefully, the reserve reindeer began his descent. He had to time it just right so that he landed on the small roof of the cottage and didn't overshoot.

"Perfect!" called the elf, as he touched down. "The first team couldn't have done better themselves, Sir!"

The reserve reindeer felt a great burst of pride as the little elf took a present from the top of the pile and slipped it down the chimney.

"You did that well, too," smiled the reindeer. "The old man

couldn't have done it better himself either!"

For the next few hours, the reindeer and the elf were so busy that they had no time to think. By the time they had delivered the last present and turned their heads towards the North Pole, they were almost asleep.

"We must be quick," yawned the elf, "so that we can get back before the others do. I'm not sure what Santa would say if he knew we had been out on our own."

Tired as he was, the reserve reindeer put every ounce of energy he possessed into the journey home. At last he saw his old home below him and coasted down to land.

No sooner had the sleigh and the reindeer touched down than the elves came running out to unharness him. There was already a faint light in the eastern sky, and on the horizon a shape could be seen, growing larger and larger. It was the returning Christmas sleigh, with Santa on board.

The elves just managed to put the elf-sleigh away as the great sleigh came in to land. The reserve reindeer barely saw it arrive. He was so tired that he simply flopped down on to his

warm straw and was asleep before his eyes had closed.

Later that night, the little reindeer dreamed that someone dressed in red was standing over him, patting his head and putting a striped blanket over him.

"Thank you, my friend," said a voice. "You have shown the true spirit of Christmas tonight."

Then the figure disappeared, and the reindeer slept on.

I expect the little reindeer *was* dreaming, for Santa never did know about the missing presents. But on Christmas morning, the reindeer found himself covered by a very special striped blanket...

The
Foolish
Fish

Long ago, in the beautiful blue waters of the Indian Ocean, there lived a very foolish fish. The only thing he was interested in was himself and how he looked.

The fish had lovely glittering scales and flashing green fins, but still he did not believe that he was beautiful enough. Some of the other fish made fun of him.

"Have you heard the latest beauty tip from the Atlantic Ocean?" one would ask another, in the hearing of the foolish fish. "They say that if you rub seaweed into your tail every day for a month, it will grow longer and shinier. I don't know if it's true."

True or not, for the next few weeks the foolish fish could be seen rubbing his tail regularly with seaweed. At the end of the month, he was quite convinced that it looked much glossier.

"What do you think?" he asked his friend, the gubble-fish. Now gubble-fish are not well known for being clever, but they do make good friends because they try to be kind all the time.

"Your tail has always been very beautiful," said the gubble-fish. "I'm sure I don't see how it could possibly have been made lovelier. But certainly, I have never seen a tail as shiny as yours is now."

The foolish fish was very pleased, but still he wished that there was some way in which he could appear even more dashing and gorgeous.

Then, one day, the fish found a casket of jewels on the sea bed. It had come from the wreck of a sailing ship hundreds of years before, but in the clear blue waters of the ocean, the jewels sparkled as if they were new. Pearls and diamonds shone and sparkled, while emeralds, rubies and sapphires glowed green, red and blue. The jewels were in the most beautiful settings, with gold and silver chains attached.

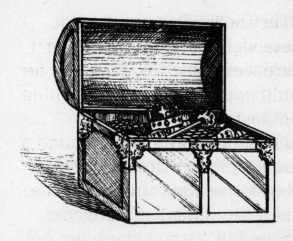

The foolish fish could not believe his eyes. Here was the answer to his prayers. If there was one thing that would make him more beautiful, it was jewellery. He looked anxiously for something that he could wear. Rubies would set off his silvery scales beautifully, but there were only brooches and necklaces, which it is difficult for fish to wear.

At last the fish spotted something absolutely right. It was a crown, with sapphires and emeralds winking around the base. And it fitted the fish perfectly!

Now fish, as you know, are not made to wear jewellery. The foolish fish found that he had to swim very, very slowly in order to stop the crown falling off. It was also quite heavy, so he found swimming hard work.

"What do you think?" he asked his fishy friends, but only the

gubble-fish had anything nice to say. The others all thought the foolish fish looked plain silly.

Now the fish loved his crown so much that he could hardly think of anything else. That is why he did not notice when all the other fish around swam quickly away one afternoon. Old man octopus was on the prowl, and it is a good idea not to come within reach of his twirly-whirly tentacles.

By the time the foolish fish noticed that the other fish had gone, it was too late. One of old man octopus's tentacles had already twisted itself around his tail, and another was wrapping itself around his silvery scales.

But as the fish wriggled in the octopus's embrace, his crown fell off into the water. The octopus, thinking it was a specially tasty snack, used two more tentacles to catch it as it drifted down and pop it into his mouth.

Have you ever seen an octopus with indigestion? It is not a pretty sight. First he went green. Then he went purple. Then he made some rather rude burping noises. At last, the pain was so bad that the octopus wrapped all of his eight tentacles around his sore tummy.

Of course, as he hugged his tummy, the octopus let go of the foolish fish, who swam away as fast as his fins would carry him.

You might think that the fish had learnt his lesson, for if the crown had not made him swim so slowly, old man octopus would never have caught him. But I'm sorry to say that he really is a very foolish fish.

"That crown saved my life!" he says to anyone who will listen.

If you see the foolish fish swimming in his new crown, you should make the most of it, for a certain eight-legged animal has a serious score to settle...

The
Invisible
Dog

One Christmas, Harry wanted one thing more than anything else. In fact, he wanted it so badly that he convinced himself he would get it for sure.

"I'm being given a dog for Christmas," he boasted to the other boys at school.

"You are not!" shouted the boys. "Your family can't afford it. Everyone knows that!"

No one liked Harry very much. He was a loner, and the other boys ignored him. Besides, he was poor and couldn't go to the cinema or the café with them.

Harry's father had been ill for a long time, and his mother could not earn very much and look after her three children as well. She knew very well what Harry wanted for Christmas, but it would be a struggle to put food on the table, never mind giving all the children expensive presents. Harry's Mum knew that there was no way her little boy's dream could come true.

But Harry was a determined little boy, and he had a strong imagination. He wasn't going to let a little thing like money stop him from having what he wanted.

When the children came back to school after Christmas, they all wanted to tell each other about the presents they had received. Harry had a smile on his face.

"Bet you didn't get a dog!" cried the other boys, but Harry only smiled.

"I did," he said. "I got the most beautiful dog you've ever seen."

"So where is it?" asked the boys with a sneer.

"You can see it tonight, if you like, when I take him for his walk," said Harry. "His name's Jack, and he's very lively."

None of the boys could believe that Harry had really been given a dog, but he seemed so certain that they began to wonder. After school, they all gathered outside Harry's house and waited for him to come out.

It was not long before Harry emerged with a rush, as though something was pulling him along. He held both his hands out in front of himself, as though he was hanging on to something for dear life. But none of the watching boys could see a dog.

"You're just pretending," they jeered. "There's no dog there!"

"Sorry," called Harry, rushing past. "I can't get him to stop! Did I mention that he's invisible?"

An invisible dog! A likely story! None of the boys believed it for a moment, but then they couldn't quite believe that Harry would pretend like this, either. Surely he must realise how silly he looked? He was much too old to have an imaginary "friend".

But Harry's belief in the dog didn't waver for a moment. Half an hour later, he returned, out of breath and muddy, looking down at his side from time to time. The dog, apparently, was walking calmly along beside him.

"I think I've tired him out," said Harry cheerfully. "See you all tomorrow! Down, Jack!"

The boys looked at each other. There wasn't a dog, was there?

Night after night, Harry left his house to take Jack for a walk.

"He's getting bigger, isn't he?" he called to the other boys. For it had become a daily habit for them to watch Harry walking his so-called invisible dog.

"One night he'll slip up," said one of the boys. "He won't come out, or he'll forget to pretend to hold the lead. Then we'll catch him out."

But Harry never forgot to hold the lead. He often bent down to pat the dog, and he talked about his Jack as proudly as any of the other boys talked about their pets. Gradually, the boys' feelings changed. They did not believe that there was a dog, but they did believe that Harry thought there was. He wasn't trying to trick them or make fun of them. He really believed that he had a dog called Jack. In a strange way, the boys began to respect the little outsider more.

One Saturday morning, the boys came across Harry running wildly down the road.

"Have you seen Jack?" he called. "Oh Jack, where are you? JACK!"

The boys could see how upset Harry was.

"Where did you see him last?" they asked.

"I took him out for a walk this morning, down to the playing field. I let him off his lead to have a run about. He started chasing birds and ran off towards the road. I haven't seen him since!" said Harry, near to tears.

"We'll help you look for him," said the boys. Then they looked at each other in confusion. How could they possibly help to find a dog they couldn't see?

But as they came round the corner towards the busy junction, Harry darted forward and knelt by the side of the road.

"Oh Jack," he sobbed, "I told you not to run out into the

traffic. Now we'll never have fun together again." And he cradled his arms around something invisible on the pavement.

"Is he…?" asked one of the boys gently.

"Yes," sobbed Harry.

"He was a wonderful dog." One of the boys put an arm around Harry's shoulder.

"I wish we could have seen him too," said another boy.

"He was the best dog ever," agreed all the others.

"Now that you don't have Jack, you'll have to play with us," suggested another boy. "But we'll never forget him, Harry."

The
Kittens
Who
Quarrelled

When Mrs Blenkinsop's cat had kittens, she intended to give them all away to good homes. The two little black and white ones found new owners very quickly, but the other two, although they were very cute and cuddly, were still at home with her after three months.

"I'm not very likely to find homes for you now," said Mrs Blenkinsop. "I suppose I shall have to keep you, although there is hardly room for three cats in my little flat."

But Mrs Blenkinsop had a little flap in her front door, so that the cat and kittens could come and go during the day, and all might have been well with her large family if only those kittens hadn't quarrelled!

It was dreadful! Night and day those two cuddly-looking kittens were arguing and fighting. If one of them wanted to play with a ball of wool, the other one wanted it. If one kitten wanted to sit on Mrs Blenkinsop's lap, the other one wanted to as well. And Mrs Blenkinsop was not a very large lady!

The kittens had a lovely basket to curl up in at night, but could they lie still until morning? Oh no! They never could agree about which was the most comfortable spot, so they were up and down, wailing and complaining, all night long.

At last Mrs Blenkinsop could stand it no longer. "If you kittens can't be friendly with each other, as sisters should be, then one of you will have to go to the cats' home and hope that they can find you a new place to live." she said crossly.

Of course, the kittens were just as quarrelsome as ever the next day, so Mrs Blenkinsop took action. She picked up the nearest kitten, popped it into a basket, and went straight down to the

cats' home as she had promised.
Mrs Blenkinsop was sorry to
say goodbye to the kitten, of
course, but she was a practical
woman. Enough was enough.
She returned home, looking
forward to a peaceful evening in
front of the television.

Oh dear! She couldn't have been more wrong! All that evening the single kitten wailed and whined. She patted Mrs Blenkinsop with her paws until the poor woman was ready to scream. And she had such a pitiful, sorrowful expression on her face that it would have broken your heart to have seen it.

Mrs Blenkinsop wasn't about to have any nonsense. "You miss your sister now," she told the kitten, "but you'll soon be used to living here with your mother. After all, you don't miss your first two sisters any more, do you? Now be a good girl."

But the little kitten did not forget. Every night, she sat right outside Mrs Blenkinsop's bedroom, making a noise that sounded for all the world like a child crying.

In the morning, the little kitten wouldn't touch her breakfast – or her supper either. She simply sat and looked up at Mrs Blenkinsop with big, sad eyes.

Mrs Blenkinsop stood it for three days and three nights. Then she could bear it no longer. She put on her hat and coat and hurried off down the road.

"I just hope I'm not too late," she muttered to herself.

Mrs Blenkinsop was breathless when she reached the cats' home.

"Have you found a home for that kitten I brought in on Tuesday?" she asked anxiously.

"Impossible!" cried the man behind the desk. "No one wants a kitten that wails all the time and won't eat."

"I do," said Mrs Blenkinsop firmly, "for I have another one just the same at home."

How happy the two kittens were to be together again – for five minutes. Then the quarrelling started again. But as Mrs Blenkinsop says, "What's a little quarrelling – between friends?"

The Forgetful Elephant

Everyone knows the old saying: an elephant never forgets. Well, that's all very well in its way, but what if you are an elephant who *does* forget? It's even worse to be forgetful if the whole world expects you to be one of those famous unforgetful types.

That was the problem with Elliot the elephant. He was an excellent fellow in every way, except that he simply could not remember things from one day to the next. He tried tying knots in his tail to remind himself, but he kept forgetting to look round and see whether his tail had knots in it – or not! He even tried tying knots in his trunk, but it was so painful that he decided even forgetting things was better than *that*.

Now it wouldn't have mattered at all if Elliot had been a warthog or a hippopotamus. No one expects them to remember anything at all. When was the last time *you* asked a warthog the date of his nextdoor neighbour's birthday? You see what I mean.

Well, almost every day of his life, one animal or another came up to Elliot and said something like this: "Elliot, you're an elephant, so you'll remember this. My friend and I can't agree whether it was last year that the waterhole was muddied by those huge hippos or the year before. Can you settle the argument?"

Ninety-nine times out of a hundred, Elliot couldn't even remember that the waterhole had been muddied, never mind which year it was. He was quite hopeless, you see.

Now, you will ask why, if all the animals knew how forgetful Elliot was, they kept asking him to remember things. What a silly question! Do you know the average memory span of a giraffe or an antelope? It's about ten minutes, which is perhaps why elephants gained such a big reputation for remembering things in the first place.

Now Elliot hated letting the other animals down, but he didn't know what to do about it. Then, one day, a little bird came and perched on his ear.

"Excuse me, Elliot," he chirped, "but you and I can help each other. I hurt my wing the other year, so I can't fly very well, and I'm frightened to bits that one of these big animals – especially the huge hippos – will tread on me one day, before I have a chance to fly away. So I was wondering if I could perch on your ear like this, and in return, I will whisper *into* your ear the answers to all the questions the animals ask you. I have an excellent memory."

Elliot agreed at once, and the plan worked perfectly. Whatever question was asked, the little bird knew the answer. He then whispered it into Elliot's ear, and Elliot boomed out the reply for all to hear. *Everyone* was happy.

What? How long was the bird's memory? Oh, about ten minutes. It was just that he was clever enough to realise that if no one *else* could remember, it didn't matter *what* he said!

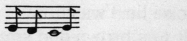

The
Bungle
Bird

Once upon a time, there was a bird that was so rare hardly anyone had ever seen it. Its name was the bungle bird. This rare bird was not very beautiful. It was brown and small. I did not have a gorgeous tail or a striped beak. In fact, to look at, it was very ordinary indeed. But the bungle bird had the most extraordinary song in the world. People who heard it declared it was like angels singing, and it is said that no one could ever be unkind or cruel again if they had once heard the bungle bird sing.

Now the bungle bird lived in a remote part of the world, but its lovely forest home was gradually destroyed by farmers and miners, until at last there were only two bungle birds left on the whole planet.

"If we stay here," said the male bungle bird, "there will be nowhere for us to raise little bungle birds. We must try to find a new home."

So the two bungle birds flew off across the forest, singing as they went. And the farmers and miners who heard them put down their tools and wept at the sound, for it was so beautiful. They vowed to harm the land no more, but the bungle birds did not know this, and they flew on.

Soon the bungle birds found themselves flying across the great ocean, where fishermen were scooping all the life from the sea.

"We will not find anywhere to build a nest here," said the female bird. "We must fly on until we reach dry land." And she flapped her wings harder, singing with all her heart as she went.

Far below on the stormy seas, the fishermen heard a sound that almost broke their hearts. They decided to stop plundering the sea of its creatures. But the bungle birds did not know this, and they flew on.

Before long, the bungle birds found themselves flying across a great city. As far as the eye could see there were buildings belching smoke and fumes.

"Oh, I can hardly breathe," coughed the male bungle bird. "We must fly farther still."

But in the dark smoke, the two birds lost sight of each other. Both of them sang and sang to try to tell the other where they were, but it was no use.

Far below, the people of the city heard music that made them want to dance and cry at the same time. They decided to do something about the horrible smoke that was filling the air. But it was too late for the last two bungle birds.

Some people say they are still flying and singing about the world, trying to find each other before it is too late. Others say that they died long ago, and it is only the echo of their song that can be heard drifting on the air.

If you go outside, and look and listen hard, you might be lucky enough to hear or see a bungle bird. If not, you will hear other birds and see other animals and plants that make you want to dance and cry. Don't let them call to you in vain...

Mr Noah's
Problem

Not many people know that
Mr Noah didn't find it easy to
invite all those animals on to his
ark. He didn't mind about the
fierce creatures, such as tigers
and big brown bears. He didn't
mind about creepy crawly
creatures, such as ants and
scorpions. He didn't even mind
about the large galumphing
animals, such as elephants and
hippopotamuses, who threatened
to unbalance the ark with every
movement of their mighty feet.
No, where Mr Noah drew the line
was at *snakes*.

"I simply can't bear those
slimy, slithery things," he said,

folding his arms. "I can't have them on the ark, and I *won't* have them on the ark. And that's all there is to it!"

But Noah was a kind man. He couldn't bear to think of any living thing suffering, so when his wife pleaded for little, harmless grass snakes, and when his sons made a good case for great big squeezing snakes, Noah allowed them on board.

"So long as I don't have to *see* them," he said, "that's all right. But those big purple and green ones are *not* coming with us. Oh no, not in a million years. I won't give them ship room."

It didn't matter how long and how hard Mrs Noah and her boys pleaded, Mr Noah had made up his mind.

"But you know you've been told to take two of *every* kind of animal," reminded his wife.

"*No one*," said Noah, "could mean to save those purple and green things. Ugh!"

Mrs Noah and the boys went into a corner and whispered together, but Mr Noah told them to hurry, for the first drops of water were falling from the sky.

For forty days and forty nights, Mr Noah and his family and all the animals floated on the flood.

Even when the rain stopped, it was a long time before they sighted land. At last the ark came to rest on a mountainside.

"Lower the gang plank!" called Noah, and his sons hauled on the thick ropes on either side of the great door.

Soon Noah and his family and all the animals stood on dry land again and praised God for saving them. A seven-coloured rainbow arched above them in the sky like a shining snake. And the great purple and green ropes that lowered the gang plank uncoiled themselves from their posts and silently slithered away.

Titles in this Series include

The Curious Kitten
The Enchanted Treasure
The Sleepy Teddy Bear
The Clever Little Rabbit
The First Little Fairy
The Elegant Elf
The Friendly Pig
The Busy Baker
The Smiling Star
The Forgetful Squirrel